Silk Umbrellas

Silk Umbrellas

CAROLYN MARSDEN

CANDLEWICK PRESS
CAMBRIDGE, MASSACHUSETTS

Copyright © 2004 by Carolyn Marsden

First paperback edition 2007

The Library of Congress has cataloged the hardcover edition as follows:
Marsden, Carolyn.
Silk umbrellas/Carolyn Marsden. — 1st ed.
p. cm.
Summary: Eleven-year-old Noi worries that she will have to stop painting the silk umbrellas her family sells at the market near their Thai village and be forced to join her older sister in difficult work at a local factory instead.
ISBN 978-0-7636-2257-2 (hardcover)
[1. Self-actualization (Psychology)—Fiction. 2. Family life—Thailand—Fiction. 3. Artists—Fiction. 4. Thailand—Fiction.] I. Title.
PZ7.M35135Si 2004
[Fic]—dc22 2003055323

ISBN 978-0-7636-3376-9 (paperback)

2 4 6 8 10 9 7 5 3 1

Printed in the United States of America

This book was typeset in Weiss.

Candlewick Press
2067 Massachusetts Avenue
Cambridge, Massachusetts 02140

visit us at www.candlewick.com

To Kanlaya Yaiprasan, in honor of
her efforts to protect the environment and
people of northern Thailand

❋ One

"Your elephant looks so alive, Kun Ya," Noi said, leaning close.

Her grandmother painted an elephant lumbering across a yellow silk umbrella. As she worked, her small body rocked with the thick, bold brush strokes.

"The eyes even sparkle," added Noi's older sister, Ting.

Noi loved to be with Kun Ya and Ting in the jungle clearing, the three of them sitting on the bamboo mat, surrounded by pots of color.

Noi dipped her fingertip into the gray, then rubbed the slick paint slowly between her thumb and forefinger.

Usually Kun Ya asked Noi and Ting to mix the paints. As Noi blended colors to create new ones, she enjoyed the way the smooth texture slipped back and forth with her brush.

Ting was content to mix paint and wash brushes, but Noi always longed to paint. Sometimes Kun Ya let her paint simple things like leaves. Noi's whole body came alive with the shades of green. Her hands felt magical when she guided the brush.

"The elephant is coming right toward us," Noi remarked. Even though she was eleven years old, she liked to pretend that Kun Ya's creatures were real.

Kun Ya laughed softly, and a breeze broke through the canopy of trees to let the sunshine in.

All morning, Noi and Ting had opened the umbrellas, getting them ready for Kun Ya's brush. They pushed the fretwork of bamboo slivers up the bamboo pole until the silk bloomed into translucent flowers of pinks, greens, purples.

Just before handing a new umbrella to Kun Ya, Noi liked to hold it up to the light, enjoying the weightless cascade of color on her face.

As Kun Ya finished, Noi carried each umbrella to the sunshine and hung it to dry. The forest floor felt soft under her bare feet.

When breezes came up, the umbrellas floated back and forth like big soft bells.

Kun Ya handed Ting the elephant umbrella. Ting stood up and twirled the umbrella overhead as she skipped around the clearing, her movements light and strong. "Look, Noi, the elephant is dancing!"

Noi laughed.

Kun Ya took up a small child's umbrella. She sketched in a pink hibiscus so quickly that it seemed as though her arm became part of the paintbrush.

Noi crouched close to watch.

Suddenly, Kun Ya held the umbrella out to Noi. "Paint a butterfly landing on the flower."

"Me?" Noi asked, staring at the green silk. A butterfly was much more complicated than simple leaves.

Kun Ya still challenged her, offering the umbrella.

"But, Kun Ya, I don't know how."

"You've watched me for years, Noi. Now try yourself."

Noi dipped the brush into the yellow. Her hand trembled as she brought the brush near the silk stretched across the bamboo frame. She glanced at the butterflies dancing close by, then began to paint yellow wings above Kun Ya's jungle flower.

"Your trembling is good, Noi," said Kun Ya. "That's the way the butterfly moves. Let the movement spread to your whole body, not just your fingers. Paint with all of you. Become the butterfly."

In an instant, Noi understood what Kun Ya meant. She sensed the butterflies hovering in the thick shade of the banana leaves, then flittering out into the sunshine. The flit of the butterflies moved into her, then out into the brush, so the paint seemed to lay itself down.

Noi held the umbrella away from her. "I did it!"

"It's pretty," said Ting.

Kun Ya smiled and began to collect the brushes, dropping them one by one into a jar of water.

Noi and Ting laid their heads down in Kun Ya's lap to wait while the umbrellas dried. Kun Ya stroked their hair and sang, "The yellow bird flies away," while Noi gazed at the flowers and creatures that Kun Ya had created. The shadows of the trees crisscrossed Kun Ya's face as she sang.

As usual, after the song was over, Noi said, "Tell me about when you were young in the jungle."

Kun Ya took a deep breath and began. "As soon as I could walk, my mother brought me to catch frogs and to gather wild mushrooms."

"Go on, tell me more." Noi knew the rest, but wanted to hear it.

"The mushrooms are still here, but the frogs have disappeared."

That part was sad to hear about, and Noi hurried the story forward. "Tell about the elephants."

"Whenever we saw elephants dragging huge teak logs through the forest, we fed them sugar cane."

"How did their trunks feel, Kun Ya? Did they grab the sugar cane from your hands?" Ting asked.

"Their trunks felt wrinkly and alive with muscles under my fingers. And yes, they snatched the sugar cane that we held out."

7

When the umbrellas were dry, Ting and Noi closed them up, the way that flowers close themselves up for the night. They put them in the basket of Kun Ya's *samlaw*, or three-wheeler.

"We worked hard today," said Kun Ya.

Kun Ya had done the real work, Noi thought. But then she recalled her butterfly umbrella, which lay in the basket with Kun Ya's umbrellas. *She* had worked too.

The large tricycle had two wheels in front with the basket between them. Behind the rider was one wheel. Kun Ya lifted her narrow sarong, climbed onto the seat, and began to pedal down the soft jungle path.

Noi ran alongside, carrying the paints and brushes. Ting followed, the bamboo mat rolled under her arm.

8

✸ Two

When the jungle parted, the house appeared, built high up on stilts to guard against flooding in the rainy season. The house had once been dark green and the big wooden shutters a rusty red, but most of the paint had flaked off in the moist jungle air.

An enormous tree spread over the front garden. Long seedpods dangled from the branches.

Noi spotted their mother to one side of the house. Her black hair tied out of the way, she hung laundry on the line, pinning it carefully while smoothing the wrinkles.

Their father was working in the space underneath the house where the pigs and chickens lived. He stirred a pot over a small fire, boiling young banana-tree shoots for the animals. His blue denim pants were rolled up around his knees as always.

"Kun Mere," Noi called out as she ran. "Kun Ya let me paint a butterfly!"

Kun Mere turned from the shirt she was hanging. "That's lovely news, Noi. Here, take this up for me." She pointed at the empty laundry basket.

Noi moved close to Kun Pa's cooking fire. The steam rising from the pot smelled like bananas. "I painted a butterfly on an umbrella!"

Kun Pa lifted the spoon from the pot and looked at Noi. "That's an honor, little daughter. Maybe you can learn to paint as well as Kun Ya does."

"Oh, Kun Pa, that would be hard!" Kun Ya didn't just decorate umbrellas; she was an artist, and her umbrellas were known throughout northern Thailand.

Yet as Noi helped Kun Ya park the tricycle under the house and put away the painting supplies, she recalled the way she had captured the butterfly with her painting, how it now lived on the green silk, landing delicately on Kun Ya's hibiscus. Her heart danced from one bit of the memory to another.

She climbed the steep wooden ladder that rose from the ground to the front door of the house. The late sunlight splashed through the door and onto the clean expanse of teakwood floor in the living room. Against the wall stood a chest carved with elephants. On it, set in frames, rested a photo of the king and queen of Thailand and another of the revered fifth king of the Chakri Dynasty, Piya Maharaj, who had abolished slavery. All around, tall windows extended from floor to ceiling.

No walls separated the living room from the cooking area, where Ting was already busy. Noi smelled the salty fish sauce that flavored almost every dish.

"Kun Ya wants to teach you to paint, Noi," said Ting, cutting a block of bean curd into cubes.

"And you, too, Ting. I'm sure she wants you to learn, too."

Ting shook her head. "No. I don't have the feeling for it, or she would have taught me

when I was your age. Here, help me chop."
She pushed several cloves of garlic and a knife
toward Noi.

It was true, thought Noi, that Ting wasn't
drawn to painting as she was.

Leaving the outer husks on the cloves, Noi
sliced them into thin ovals. Out the window,
she watched Kun Pa feeding the pigs far below.
They gathered around him, pushing at his legs
with their snouts, squealing as the boiled banana
stems fell into the carved wooden trough.

Ting scooped the garlic slices into a pan of
hot oil, added eggs, then stirred quickly. She
hummed a little song under her breath as she
worked.

Noi took the empty egg basket and put it
near the door, then swept the wooden floor,
reaching the broom into the corners. When

she was finished, she laid out the large mat for eating, making sure that it was straight and even.

Kun Pa came up the ladder into the house, his empty cooking pot banging against the rungs. "Today those animals were acting like Srithon's children," he remarked. Srithon, who lived across the village, had ten children, all boys. They impolitely took large servings of food onto their plates.

Kun Pa loved to joke. At dinner he liked to be entertained. Maybe he would like to see the green umbrella, Noi thought. She would show him and Kun Mere the butterfly.

But when Kun Mere and Kun Ya came up the ladder, they were whispering together. Did they have a troubling secret? Kun Ya's wrinkles looked deeper, and the corners of Kun Mere's mouth were pinched tight.

14

Later, thought Noi, *I'll bring out the umbrella later.*

Everyone sat down cross-legged on the mat and passed the bowl of rice, bean curd and pork cooked with garlic, the flat yellow omelet, and the tiny dish of fish sauce and chili.

Kun Pa didn't seem to notice that Kun Mere and Kun Ya looked serious. "Srithon's poor wife," he said, serving himself a piece of omelet. "She keeps only female animals to save herself from going crazy with so many boys." He ate slowly, clacking his big spoon against the dish. His work with Mr. Khayan had started early that morning.

When Noi was young, Kun Pa had planted the fields he rented from the landlord. Every night he came home with baskets of vegetables. Noi remembered washing the dirt off the crinkly cabbage leaves and snaky green beans as long as her forearm. When it was rice harvest, they'd always had fragrant jasmine rice to eat. Noi had helped Kun Mere pick out the bad grains that floated to the top when the rice was rinsed.

Kun Pa used to load the back of a little truck with the harvest and take it to market to sell. He returned from the market with coconut treats for Ting and Noi. They'd waited for him to come back and had jumped up and down at the sight of him, their mouths eager for the sweetness.

They'd had all they could eat, and not much need of money to spend.

Then suddenly the landlord had sold the farmland to a company that built vacation houses for city people and foreigners. Kun Pa and the other small farmers had had to find jobs. Now Kun Pa worked for the construction foreman, Mr. Khayan, laying bricks for those houses. But work was available only now and then.

"Work for Mr. Khayan?" Kun Mere had said at first. "How can you work for someone who's destroying the farmland?" But in the end, Kun Mere, who kept the family budget, agreed that laying bricks was the only thing for Kun Pa to do. Throughout the village, women were in charge of all such household decisions.

Now whenever Kun Pa touched Noi, she felt how his hands had grown cracked and dry from handling the mortar. And in the evenings, Noi overheard him and Kun Mere talking about not having enough money.

◆ ◆ ◆

Tonight Kun Mere said nothing when Kun Pa
left after dinner to play chess with his friends.
Usually, she would tease him a little about
leaving. "Aren't you going to the cockfights
instead?" she might say. But tonight, Noi noticed that Kun Mere let him depart in peace.

Kun Ya, saying she was tired from the sun,
went to her room.

Noi, Ting, and Kun Mere remained together
on the mat, even though they'd finished eating. Usually, the three of them would get up
and work quickly to gather and wash the dishes.
But tonight something unspoken held them
still. What had Kun Mere and Kun Ya been
whispering about?

The room was lit with one bare bulb. It
cast a bright light but also harsh shadows.

"Please clean up tonight, Noi. Ting and I have to talk," said Kun Mere, uncrossing and crossing her legs with the opposite one on top. She looked down, her face washed with shadow.

Noi gathered the dishes. She tried to steady them, since their clatter sounded huge in the silence of the room.

Ting sat with her hands folded. Outside, thousands of crickets sounded together with one voice.

"Ting, I've arranged the job for you," said Kun Mere as soon as Noi had cleared the eating mat.

"Is it the factory job?" Ting asked. Kun Mere had been talking about this job for weeks.

Noi filled the large bowl from a jar of rainwater, pouring smoothly, just as Kun Mere's words poured out as though she had already practiced saying them.

"Yes, making radios. Many of my friends in this village have sons and daughters in the factory. It isn't so bad."

Ting said nothing.

The crickets' song grew louder.

Noi glanced to see Ting trace the lines on the palms of her hands with her fingertip, as she did whenever she was distressed.

The factory. If Ting worked there, she wouldn't be able to help Noi and Kun Ya with the umbrellas.

"You'll make money for the family. Your father and I won't have to worry so much."

That would be good, Noi thought. Her parents could talk about something else in the evenings for once.

"But, Kun Mere, I've heard that the chemicals make the workers sick," Ting said. "And looking at the tiny parts for so long damages the eyesight."

Noi plunged her hands into the cool water. Was the factory job a bad one, then? Surely, hearing that, Kun Mere would change her mind. She might say, "Well, never mind, then, I'll find you something else," and ask Ting to help her fold up the eating mat.

"If that were true, my friends would have told me about it," Kun Mere continued instead. "Tomorrow the bus will pick you up."

Noi turned to look at Kun Mere. Was she joking? Did she have a playful smile on her face? But Kun Mere's face was down, her expression shadowed.

✳ Three

When Noi heard the first birds calling to each other across the jungle, she got up. She tied back the mosquito net, shook out the sleeping mat that she shared with Ting, then folded it into a neat pile against the wall. She opened the tall shutters to the trees outside. There was no glass in the windows, and the enormous banana leaves pressed close.

Ting had already left, headed for the bus stop and her first day at the factory.

In bed last night, Ting had whispered, "The factory might be fun. I'll meet new people. I'll earn money. Maybe I'll even buy you something special."

Noi had said, "Yes, it might be good." But she couldn't forget what Ting had said about the factory workers getting sick.

The sun rose, pulling a curtain of light across the sky.

In the bathroom stood a tall black jar of rainwater. Noi used the clear surface of the water as a mirror. Each morning before she bathed, she leaned over to look at her light skin, her thin arched eyebrows, and her straight, even teeth stained ever so slightly. Kun Ya said that the stains came from minerals in the drinking water.

23

Noi plunged a dipper into the water, then lifted it to splash herself clean. After she'd bathed, she combed out her long black hair, then twisted it into a bun at the back of her head.

She dressed in her uniform of a blue skirt and crisp white blouse. *I won't be wearing this much longer*, she thought, pulling the collar straight. Because she was eleven years old, this would be her last year of school. Most children in the village didn't study beyond grade school.

Ting had been out of school for four years.

The house smelled of the morning incense that burned in a smoky plume from the altar high on the wall, where a wooden Buddha sat, his palms facing upward, his eyes downcast.

"*Sawasdee*, little daughter." Kun Mere said

good morning as though nothing had happened the night before.

"*Sawasdee*, Kun Mere," Noi answered. Surely, Kun Mere knew the right thing to do with Ting. Hadn't she tended the altar, placing fresh flowers and food and lighting the incense stick? Surely she was in harmony with the Buddha and would never do anything against his holy principles.

After breakfast, Kun Mere settled down to her sewing machine. She turned on the lamp and pushed the sewing machine pedal with the tip of her toe, making mosquito nets, the netted fabric billowing around her.

Once a week, Mr. Subsin collected the nets, carrying them to other villages to sell.

He loaded the bundles into his tiny truck and took off, the jungle caressing the fenders, black smoke puffing from the exhaust pipe.

By sewing mosquito nets, Kun Mere brought a little money into the household.

Noi descended the wooden ladder. In the dim green light underneath the house rested the umbrellas that she and Kun Ya had worked on the day before, piled in neat stacks, waiting to go to the Saturday tourist market.

The butterfly umbrella lay somewhere in those stacks. Would Kun Ya include that umbrella when the others went to market? Was it good enough to sell?

The tricycle was already loaded with fresh umbrellas. Noi laid her hand on the top one, the silk cool against her palm. Today in the jungle, Kun Ya might paint colorful parrots with airy flicks of her wrist.

Noi walked alone to school, following the narrow forest path until it opened onto the road leading into the village. Ahead of her, a boy rode his bicycle, reaching up with one arm to touch the feathery archway of trees.

Noi walked slowly, stopping every now and then to look up. Above the canopy, clouds gathered, their misty whiteness forming out of the pale blue sky. She imagined mixing blues and greens and pure white to paint that sky.

No rain would fall yet, but the clouds signaled the end of the dry season.

When Noi rounded the last bend, the temple appeared before her. Even though she'd seen it all her life, she always caught her breath a little at the sight of the gigantic golden cone rising out of the trees. Built by an ancient king, the temple was covered with jewels and flashed brilliantly in the sunshine.

27

In contrast, the school attached to the golden temple was a rough wood building.

As Noi entered the grassy field in front of the school, she stooped to pet the temple cats and dogs. A tiger cat rubbed against her while a rooster ran screeching, chased by a black dog with short legs.

"*Sawasdee*, Kun Kru," Noi said to her teacher at the top of the steps. She bowed to Kun Kru with the palms of her hands pressed together in front of her heart.

"*Sawasdee*, Nuan-noi." Only her teacher called Noi by her full name. Kun Kru was dressed in a plain dark blue dress, her hair pinned neatly at the back of her head. She'd arrived just this year from a teachers college in Bangkok, the big city to the south.

At the top of the stairs, Noi slipped off her sandals and entered the classroom.

Intha and another boy, Go, had already arrived and laid out copybooks on their desks. Children of all ages came to the one big room to be taught by Kun Kru. Soon Jirapat and her brother, Thongin, his slingshot in his back pocket as usual, seven of Srithon's ten boys, and Noi's special friend, Kriamas, appeared.

Kriamas waved to Noi, then leaned forward to unload her satchel, her black hair falling over her cheeks.

Kun Kru, as always, had written sayings from the Buddha on the blackboard in her careful rendering of the swirls and curls of the Thai alphabet.

Noi opened her book and began to copy the sacred words. She enjoyed the copying, because it reminded her of painting. She made sure that the words looked nice on the page.

The moist air blew through the spaces between the rough-cut boards, ruffling Noi's paper. In the temple, Noi heard the comforting drone of the monks chanting.

In spite of the early hour, the air hung close and steamy. Noi wiped her face with a clean square of cloth from her pocket. Each time new children arrived, the room grew hotter.

Noi finished and waited for Kun Kru to collect her book. She was happy with her neat penmanship. She smiled across the room at Kriamas, who also worked hard. Kriamas planned to become a teacher like Kun Kru.

Kun Kru motioned, and the children stood to recite the morning poem, which began:

Having knowledge is like having great wealth;
You will never lack wherever you go.

As Noi sat back down, she wondered how Ting was doing in the factory. Did the poem tell the truth—was the knowledge that Ting had gained in school helping in her new job? At the factory, was it useful that she could copy the holy words of the Buddha with perfect lettering?

❊ Four

That evening Noi sat with Kun Mere before
the tall window with the shutters open, waiting
for Ting to come home. Kun Mere embroidered
a cloth with red thread. Soon the factory bus
would arrive and Ting would run along the
lane, her footsteps quick on the soft dirt.

Gradually, dusk gathered under the trees,
then entered the room, coming between Kun

Mere and Noi. Birds flew from tree to tree, preparing for the night.

Noi slapped at the mosquitoes that came out after sunset and bit her ankles. Her palms reddened with blood. Why was Ting so late?

The jungle grew velvety black and the *hinghoy*, or fireflies, began to appear, zigzagging through the bushes, making the trees pulse with light. Sometimes Noi liked to catch one and hold it, glowing, in her hands. But tonight she could think only of seeing Ting.

Kun Mere turned on the light behind them in the living room, illuminating the house and even a little distance into the jungle. Yet still no Ting.

When Ting did arrive, Noi didn't hear her footsteps on the path but rather sensed her presence at the bottom of the ladder. She went to the top rung. "Ting?"

Silence.

"Ting, is that you?"

"Yes, Noi." Ting exhaled the words.

"What's wrong?"

"I'm tired, that's all." With that, Ting climbed the ladder, emerging into the range of the light. She stood a minute, silhouetted in the doorway, her shape dark against the dark.

Kun Mere set aside her embroidery, and Noi stepped backward.

Stray pieces of Ting's curly hair wandered loose from her comb. The pupils of her eyes were large and black.

Kun Mere gestured toward the eating mat that Noi had left out for Ting.

"Sit down," said Kun Mere.

Ting sat, crossing her legs in front of her.

"How was the work, little daughter?" Kun

Mere asked brightly, arranging Ting's dinner in a bowl and setting it in front of her on the mat.

Outside, an owl hooted—two long, smooth notes—then silence. Inside, a mosquito whined.

Noi reached into her book bag and took out a schoolbook. She opened it and pretended to read.

Ting paused for so long before answering that Noi finally looked up.

The owl hooted again.

Would Ting refuse to answer Kun Mere?

At last she said, "I did the same thing all day. I used tweezers to balance a tiny part on a wire. Then I used a small tool to solder the part on."

"Was that all?"

"Yes, Kun Mere." Ting lifted her bowl of noodle soup close to her face and began to spoon it into her mouth quickly.

Noi stared at her book. She'd never seen Ting so tired. Did Kun Mere really know what she was doing? The words on the page crowded together and drifted apart without making sense.

After they were both in bed, the mosquito net drawn and tucked tightly, Noi reached for Ting's hand. "How was it really?"

Ting yawned so hugely that Noi felt her moist breath on her cheek. "Very boring. You wouldn't like it."

"But do *you*?"

"It'll do for now," Ting said. And then she was asleep, her hand limp in Noi's.

As Noi lay awake, turning Ting's new life over and over in her mind, she overheard Kun Ya talking with Kun Mere in the kitchen.

"That factory isn't a good place for a young girl. It will cost her her health and youth."

Kun Mere was silent.

"She shouldn't have to go, my daughter," Kun Ya insisted, her voice as muscular as her strong fingers.

"I would go in her place, but the work needs a young person's perfect eyes and steady hands," said Kun Mere.

A painful silence followed.

Noi smelled smoke. Kun Ya had rolled a cigar from fresh tobacco leaves and was smoking, as she did whenever she wanted to think.

"You must understand, Kun Mere," Kun Mere finally addressed her mother. "Without

37

her work, we don't have enough." Her words sounded like coins being counted out one by one.

Ting turned her head back and forth on her pillow. No one ever talked against the advice of the household elder.

The smoke from Kun Ya's cigar made Noi sneeze. She muffled the sneeze with the blanket so that no one would know she was awake.

"There must be other ways," Kun Ya finally said.

The aching silence. Noi wished the owl would hoot again to break it.

✽ Five

Early Saturday morning, Kun Ya and Noi gathered the painted umbrellas and loaded them into the basket of the tricycle. Noi noticed that Kun Ya added her butterfly umbrella to the stack.

"Will we sell it, then?" she asked shyly.

"Why not?" Kun Ya asked. "It's beautiful."

Noi felt a sudden longing to keep the umbrella. After all, the butterfly was the first thing she'd painted other than leaves.

Kun Ya must have understood what she was thinking. "Don't worry, little daughter, there's plenty more where that came from. Here"—she touched the area over Noi's heart—"and here." She touched Noi's hands.

Noi felt a quick flush of warmth. She wanted Kun Ya to say more, but she had already mounted the tricycle and was pedaling away.

"Ting won't be going with us anymore, will she?" Noi called out.

"I'm afraid not, Noi. Now she has to work on Saturdays."

Sadness passed over Noi like a cool wind.

Once again, Noi ran alongside Kun Ya as she rode. Whenever the road went downhill, Noi put her feet on the back step of the tricycle and caught a lift as the *samlaw* coasted.

As they approached the tourist market, they reached the main highway. It was always clogged with a snarl of trucks and buses. Curls of black smoke rose and mingled together to form a haze. Noi covered her ears against the roar.

People pedaled bicycles or tricycles like their own, or rode in the beds of small trucks. The tourists arrived in big buses or in cars.

Some of the tourists were Thais from Bangkok. Others came from Japan. But the market was held mostly for the *farangs* from Europe and America. Each Saturday, Noi tried hard not to stare at these tall people with round eyes and light hair and skin.

Monks also wandered through the market, their rubber sandals clicking against their heels.

Kun Ya and Noi pushed the tricycle into the narrow lane of the market. They passed under the canvas awning that spread over the market to keep out the sun and, in the rainy season, the rain. Alongside the lanes were booths of things for sale: carved wooden elephants and water buffalo, silver bowls engraved with classic Thai designs, elephant bells, woven napkins and pillowcases, kites made of bamboo and paper, bamboo baskets, rolls of fluttering silk, landscapes embroidered with colorful yarn, Thai swords in sheaths. Several booths sold umbrellas, but none were as finely painted as Kun Ya's.

As Kun Ya wheeled the tricycle through the market with Noi following, women called out to her. "Sell your umbrellas here today," or "We'll give you the best price."

But Kun Ya just laughed at the teasing. For

many years, she'd sold her umbrellas only to Mr. Poonsub.

When they got to Mr. Poonsub's booth, Noi greeted him: *"Sawasdee."* She bowed deeply, because Mr. Poonsub was almost as old as Kun Ya. His short, round fingers were heavy with silver rings.

"Sawasdee." Mr. Poonsub bent low to Kun Ya and glanced toward Noi.

As Kun Ya and Noi took the umbrellas from the basket, Mr. Poonsub opened them one by one, sometimes saying nothing, sometimes exclaiming. When he got to the green child's umbrella, Noi held her breath. But he barely opened it and seemed to accept it like all the others. After he had examined all of the umbrellas, he counted paper money and ten-*baht* coins into Kun Ya's open hands.

At a stand, Kun Ya bought Noi a cup of

coconut-flavored drink. Noi sipped it carefully as they walked, letting the slippery pieces of coconut glide into her mouth. She liked to suck the sweetness out before swallowing.

At home, Kun Ya gave ten *baht* to Noi and most of the paper money to Kun Mere. Kun Ya always kept a few notes for herself.

Noi opened the lid of a tiny wooden box and placed the ten-*baht* coin inside with the others.

✸ Six

Noi woke to the sound of downpour. Rain-drops landed heavily on the banana leaves outside the window. She shivered and pulled her cotton blanket higher over her shoulders. School would be closed with such heavy rain falling.

Ting's side of the bed was empty. Noi got up quickly and opened the shutters just in time to see her sloshing to the bus even though the rain fell like a great gray waterfall. Ting held a banana leaf over her head with one hand and carried her lunch box in the other. Noi watched until she disappeared.

Kun Ya came up quietly behind Noi. She rested her hands on Noi's shoulders. "It's not good to go out in the rain. She's too young to do that."

"You're up so early, Kun Ya." Noi turned and put her arms around Kun Ya's neck. Under her forearms, she felt Kun Ya's thin shoulder blades, like wings, beneath her sleeping dress. "I wish Ting didn't have to go to the factory."

"I know, little daughter."

"Please do something for her, Kun Ya."

"At one time I would have had that power, Noi. Things are changing." She put a cool hand against Noi's cheek.

Noi could hear Kun Ya's heart beating

through the thin fabric—a sound like a far-away drumbeat.

Kun Ya's chest lifted as she said, "Since you can't go to school, let's paint together inside near the big window."

Just then, the sun broke through the clouds, shining brilliantly through the cascade of rain.

After breakfast, Noi put on her plastic raincoat and went down the ladder, the rain thudding on her head and back as she descended. At ground level, the water already rose ankle deep. Underneath the house, she gathered an armful of umbrellas and pulled herself up, rung by rung, with her free arm.

She went back down to collect the basket of paints and brushes.

Noi spread the mat and laid out the umbrellas. Kun Ya sat down and slowly took an umbrella into her hand. "We must be still for a moment, Noi, and listen to the umbrella. Look at its color and the way the light touches it. Know the story it wants you to tell before you begin."

Kun Ya started to paint a quiet scene of lily pads. Then she turned and placed the umbrella in Noi's hands. "Here, finish it for me, little daughter. The damp air makes me sleepy."

Noi could see that Kun Ya had meant to continue the lily pads around the edge of the umbrella, making them grow smaller and smaller. She had watched her create this design before. But completing this painting was a far larger task than painting the butterfly.

"You know how, Noi. It's time for you to go further," Kun Ya said softly.

The thunderous beating on the tin roof almost hid her words.

After Noi had finished the lily pads, her body full of the roundness of them, she turned to show her work to Kun Ya. But Kun Ya had lain down on her side and now slept. Noi crawled inside of the mosquito net. She pressed her face close to Kun Ya's hair, which smelled of fresh lemongrass, and sang "Yellow Bird" very softly.

From the kitchen, Noi heard the sound of one of Ting's radios. The singer sang of lost love. Tiny bells played like drops of water falling.

❃ Seven

"Oh, look, Noi. Ting went off without taking her lunch," Kun Mere said one afternoon after school.

The lunch box sat on the kitchen worktable, a stack of three metal bowls clamped together, one on top of the other. Noi knew that the bottom bowl held rice; the middle, vegetables and slivers of pork; and the top, chunks of fresh pineapple. Ting would be hungry.

"I can take it to her," said Noi. "The rain has stopped."

"But the factory is a long distance and on a busy road," said Kun Mere.

Noi knew that it was Mr. Subsin's day to come for the mosquito nets and that Kun Mere was anxious to finish sewing. "I can go."

The lunch box clattered in the basket of the bicycle as Noi rode over the bumpy forest path. She traveled through the village, past her school and the temple, following the map that Kun Mere had sketched. One of the temple dogs chased her, yipping at the tires.

Finally, she reached the highway. Instead of going into the market as usual, she turned onto the shoulder of the busy road. Some-times when the big trucks passed her they honked, and the wind they created blew hard against her.

When Noi arrived at the plain factory building, she parked the bicycle. The building had no windows. Walking up the front steps, she carried the lunch box, the handle square and hard against her palm.

"How can I help you?" A man in a white uniform opened the door and stood above her. He had a badge pinned to his shirt pocket.

"I brought my sister's lunch." Noi held up the metal stack.

"It's past lunchtime," the man said.

"But she's probably hungry."

The man looked at his watch. "Okay. They get a short break soon." He reached for the lunch box, but Noi held on to it.

"I'd like to take it to her, please." She wanted to make sure that Ting got the lunch, and besides, now that she'd come this long distance, she wanted to see where Ting worked.

"This way, then," the man said, holding the door open wider. Noi passed in and followed him down a short hallway. On the wall hung photographs of the king and queen. The hallway led into a large room lit by cold-looking lights. There were four rows of workers, about ten in a row. At first, Noi couldn't spot Ting, because each young worker had the same black hair pulled into a net and each wore a pair of thick magnifying glasses. A wide moving belt ran in front of each row. Metal boxes sprouting tangles of wires passed along the belt.

She saw Ting bent over the belt like the other workers, accepting each box as it came to her. In front of her rested a cup filled with small bits of something. Noi scarcely breathed as she watched Ting lift the bit with a pair of tweezers and maneuver it onto the box. When the piece was settled, she used a tool that looked like a pen with an electrical cord attached and glued the piece on. All the while, the box had been moving toward her, in front of her, and then away from her.

Except for the rhythmical spinning of the overhead fans and the ringing of the phones down the hall, there was no sound. None of the workers talked. Even the light was unwavering, as though the least flicker might disrupt the delicate work. Noi shut her eyes briefly. How could Ting do this all day long?

She went up behind her and whispered, "I've brought your lunch."

"Thank you, Noi," Ting said without looking up.

Noi saw that she couldn't look up. If she did, her unit wouldn't receive its piece and the next worker couldn't do her job. The belt would have to stop.

How different this was from the days with the umbrellas—filled with light and shadow, breezes and laughter.

Noi let her gaze shift from Ting to the others bent over their tasks. Most looked to be Ting's age, out of school for a few years. But then she looked more closely. Some workers were younger than Ting. Some were very young. They looked almost as young as Noi herself.

Suddenly, she understood—she, too, was destined to come here to the factory, to work here with the radios day in and day out. She might come as soon as she finished school.

After all, why not? Why should she, and not Ting, be spared? Why would Kun Mere wait? Even with Ting working, Kun Mere and Kun Pa still worried about money.

School would be over soon, and then the metal boxes would begin to move toward her, on and on without stopping.

Her stomach tightened, then loosened quickly, as though she would be sick. She turned to the guard. "I want to leave now."

The man led her back down the hall and outside again.

Noi stood by the bicycle, gulping in the cool, fresh air. She felt the sky open above her, the land stretch away on all sides. How could Ting bear to be locked up?

As she mounted the bicycle, she thought about the time a boy had brought a toy called a kaleidoscope to school. When Noi looked through it, she'd seen the world broken apart and rearranged in beautiful patterns.

Now that she'd visited the factory, the whole world seemed broken into pieces like that. But unlike the view through the kaleidoscope, the broken pieces didn't make lovely patterns.

✳ Eight

That evening Noi and Ting prepared to iron clothes with the charcoal iron. The iron had a hollow space underneath the handle. Noi held the iron close to the cooking fire, a cloth wrapped around the handle to shield her hand from the heat. Ting used a pair of tongs to lift hot coals into the opening.

Noi held the iron very still, even though she was trembling inside with the question she was about to ask.

When the iron was filled with coals and the lid was latched closed, Ting set it on the thick blanket spread out on the floor.

Noi handed her Kun Pa's brown shirt from the basket. Now was the time to ask. She had to know for sure. Her words rushed out: "Do you think that Kun Mere means to send me to the factory, too?"

"Don't worry yourself about that now," said Ting. She looked quickly at Noi, then back to the shirt collar she was straightening.

But Noi pushed on. "Has she said anything to you?"

"Not directly." Ting bit her lip. "But probably yes, I think she plans to send you."

Noi's hand brushed the hot iron, and she jerked it back. Her skin bubbled right away into a blister.

"Put some oil on that," said Ting.

Noi dabbed on cooking oil from the nearby jar. Tears came to her eyes and rolled down her cheeks as pain rushed at her from all directions.

"Does your hand hurt very badly?" Ting asked, touching the red spot lightly with her fingertip.

"Yes," said Noi, although the blister itself was only a small part of the hurt. The wound had forced her deeper anguish into the open.

She watched Ting finish the brown shirt, running the iron up and down one sleeve, then turning the shirt to line up the other sleeve. Ting hung the shirt neatly on a hanger, then began on a flower-print dress of Kun Mere's.

"And what about you, Ting? You act as though you don't mind the factory," Noi finally managed to say.

"I don't mind too much. I'm not like you."

"But the factory looked so…" Noi wanted to go on and, sobbing, tell Ting what she'd observed at the factory and all about the kaleidoscope of broken parts her life had become. But she stopped, not wanting to make Ting feel bad.

Ting moved the iron over Kun Mere's pale flowers, the point traveling first, then the triangular body. "Really, I'm fine," she said as she finished the dress. "For now, Kun Mere needs me to work there."

The rainy season had never seemed longer, nor the rainfall more torrential. Often there was no school because of the rain, so Noi stayed home. When she did go, she had trouble concentrating on what Kun Kru taught her.

Because of the rain, Kun Pa couldn't lay bricks. He sat in the house weaving bamboo fishing baskets, the long strips of bamboo uncurling on the mat.

Kun Mere's sewing machine whirred along except when lightning hit the electrical wires. Then Noi would light a lantern. She brought it close so that Kun Mere could continue to sew by hand with tiny, neat stitches.

Kun Ya slept and hardly painted at all. She complained that her fingers hurt.

Only Ting kept to her schedule in spite of the weather, slipping out of the mosquito net before dawn each morning. Every other Friday, she handed Kun Mere her earnings. They sat down together on the mat while Ting, smiling, counted the bills and coins into Kun Mere's open hand. Kun Mere would count the money again, then neatly enter the amount in a small notebook. Often Ting's money was the only money coming into the house.

Noi stayed busy with schoolwork and housework, trying to avoid Kun Mere's eyes.

As the rains crashed down day after day, Noi began to look ahead to the harvest festival of Loy Krathong.

During Loy Krathong, people celebrated the life of all growing things. The harvest brought new prosperity. Noi hoped that the festival celebrations would bring prosperity for her family. Maybe there would be enough money so that neither she nor Ting would have to go to the factory.

During Loy Krathong, the village would be lit up by *phang patit*, the small earthen lamps. Noi added up the number of lamps her family would light. She was eleven years old, Ting fifteen. That made twenty-six. Plus Kun Mere's thirty-five years and Kun Pa's thirty-seven made ninety-eight. Plus Kun Ya's sixty-three years made one hundred and sixty-one. The flickering yellow flames of one hundred and sixty-one lamps would make the fall night seem warmer.

Noi pictured the lights that would burn under the trees around the house. She counted them over and over until the individual flickers came clear. The thought of so many lights, small offerings to the Buddha, comforted her.

❋ Nine

Noi approached Kun Mere's sewing machine. She touched the soft cloud of mosquito netting hesitantly.

Recently a curtain had come between her and Kun Mere like the thin white fabric Kun Mere used to make mosquito nets. The curtain made it impossible for Noi to speak the secrets of her heart.

Kun Mere didn't lift her foot from the pedal of the sewing machine. She leaned close to the fabric, pulling it tight on both sides of the needle that jabbed up and down, joining the seams.

Kun Mere used to have time to sew blouses with pleats and ruffles for Noi and Ting, but now she only sewed for Mr. Subsin.

Noi began to move away.

"Wait, little daughter." Kun Mere suddenly took a pink ribbon from her pocket.

Noi leaned down to let Kun Mere tie the ribbon in her hair.

Kun Mere pulled at the collar of Noi's blouse. "I see wrinkles. You need to iron more carefully in the future."

Noi smiled. Even if Kun Mere didn't have time to sew blouses, she always made sure that Noi and Ting looked neat and pretty.

But looks didn't matter to Noi right now. *Find another way. Please, don't send me to the factory,* she longed to say to Kun Mere.

Yet she didn't say anything. Neither did she lean over to kiss Kun Mere as she usually did. She pretended to be late for school and turned quickly to gather up her book bag.

Kun Kru handed out the mathematics books for the older children and drew the younger ones close to her for reading.

As Noi added and subtracted fractions and decimals, she wondered what these complicated numbers had to do with the numbers in her life—the simple, round numbers on the money that Ting brought home, the lack of simple, round numbers that so worried Kun Mere.

Noi looked out the window just in time to see a monk striking the big gong in the courtyard. He raised the mallet. *Bong* ... The sound resonated throughout the village, marking the hour of eleven o'clock. It was time for the monks to eat.

Kun Kru dismissed the younger children.

Noi slipped her mathematics paper inside her book and closed it, as though in so doing she could put away numbers and the problems they created.

The monks had to eat before noon, but the children would eat later. Outside, Kun Kru lined everybody up for a foot race.

Kriamas liked to run fast. Noi preferred to go slower, feeling the breeze on her face, watching the rush of the green trees against the background of sky.

It was the same way in the afternoons

when Kun Kru announced the end of work and the beginning of the performances. Kriamas enjoyed doing her dances or singing in front of the others, while Noi enjoyed studying the way the children moved and the positions of their bodies, thinking how, like the creatures of the jungle, they could be painted.

Everyone shared some lunch with everyone else, making a feast of Jirapat's yellow curried potatoes with chickpeas, Intha's crispy raw vegetables, Kriamas's rice soup. Afterward, Kriamas and Noi played a game of checkers, using bottle caps for pieces. In the background, a Ping-Pong ball clicked back and forth, a pattern threading lightly through the laughter and chatter.

Noi took three of Kriamas's pieces and Kriamas grew quiet. She began to move, then changed her mind.

Noi rubbed her finger around the fluted edge of the bottle cap. She wished that she could tell Kriamas about the factory. About the way Ting rubbed her eyes at night. About how Noi's school days seemed to fly by, as time carried her swiftly to a new destiny. *I'm so afraid*, she wanted to say.

But Kriamas's father had his own land and still farmed. The family had money to send Kriamas to teacher school. Because Kriamas didn't have to think about the factory, she might not understand.

Kriamas moved and it was Noi's turn.

Noi lifted her own piece just when Kun Kru rang her brass bell, announcing the beginning of afternoon studies.

✻ Ten

"Let's go to market," Kun Pa announced one morning when the rain had broken. He had loaded the *samlaw* with a tall stack of fishing baskets. The fishing baskets would bring more money at the tourist market than if he sold them to the men of the village. The baskets would never catch fish, but would hold tourist trinkets instead.

There were no umbrellas to load, because Kun Ya hadn't been painting. Noi thought of the umbrellas she'd decorated with lily pads. But Mr. Poonsub wouldn't buy *those*.

She climbed onto the back step of the tricycle.

Before Ting had gone to the factory, Noi would have held on to Kun Pa's shoulders as he pedaled. She'd have leaned over, the side of her head against his, laughing as he took the turns too fast.

When Noi was little, Kun Pa had carried her high on his shoulders through the jungle. They'd made a game of spotting the bright-colored birds that were now calling their morning greeting. "There's one!" she'd cry at seeing a flash of feathers against the green. When Kun Pa grew tired of carrying her, they walked with her small hand in his big one.

Sometimes she'd asked him to tell the story of the poisonous king cobras. When Kun Pa was her age, he'd spotted two shiny black snakes slithering through the grass outside his house. Fascinated, little Kun Pa had laughed brightly and chased after them.

Just as the snakes turned and opened the hoods around their heads, Kun Pa's mother had scooped him up in her arms and hoisted him above the snakes. "Those might have killed you, Chang-noi!" She always called him "Little Elephant."

At that point in his story, Kun Pa had always lifted Noi high, provoking a shower of giggles.

But Kun Pa had played with Ting as well. He'd called Ting his precious little daughter, had stroked her hair as she fell asleep with her head against his shoulder, had told her, too, about the snakes. And he'd still let Kun Mere send her to the factory.

Now, instead of leaning close to Kun Pa as she rode on the back step of the *samlaw*, Noi held him at the waist with only her hands touching his shirt.

On the way to the booth that bought and sold fishing baskets, they passed Mr. Poonsub's booth.

"Where are your grandmother's umbrellas?" he asked. "People have been wanting them, and they're all gone." He spread his hands, indicating the lack of umbrellas, his rings flashing.

"Kun Ya has been feeling tired because of the rains."

"I'm sorry to hear that. Please take her

this." He folded up a square of white silk and wrapped it in paper.

"Thank you, Mr. Poonsub," said Noi, taking the package.

"She's not painting, but *you* could paint, no?" Mr. Poonsub laughed.

"I'm not sure, Mr. Poonsub," Noi said very quietly. How did he know about the little things Kun Ya had asked her to paint? Was he only joking, or did he think she could paint umbrellas so beautifully that he would buy them?

If he bought them, she would earn money for the household....

Just then, Noi saw a booth selling radios in rows, all exactly alike, smooth and cold-looking. She wondered if they were the radios that Ting made.

The sight of the radios made Noi slow

down. They seemed out of place in the market. The other goods—Kun Ya's umbrellas, the wooden carvings, the embroidered cloths—were all made by people. The radios looked as if they were made by machines.

But the radios *were* made by people, part of her argued. Hadn't she seen Ting and the others putting them together?

Noi turned her eyes away. She'd walk in the other direction next time.

✸ Eleven

Kun Ya slept for three whole days.

Noi opened the mosquito net and searched for insects that might disturb her sleep. Gently, she massaged the beautiful wrinkles on the backs of Kun Ya's hands. She thought over and over about what Mr. Poonsub had said. He must have been joking, of course. But his joke made her consider: Hadn't

Kun Ya asked her to paint the butterfly and then the lily pads?

She wished that Kun Ya would wake up and help her.

On the third day, Noi took an umbrella of a soft brown color. She closed her eyes and listened for the scene as Kun Ya had taught her. She saw Kun Ya holding a stick of sugar cane out to an elephant. The elephant reached with its trunk.

Oh, but an elephant! How could the umbrella have asked her to paint something so difficult!

Slowly, Noi mixed different shades of gray in the bowls. The vision of the elephant had come to her, but she was afraid of spoiling the umbrella.

She closed her eyes again and looked inside until she could see the elephant in the jungle, could hear its thick feet in the long grass, the small snorts it made with its trunk.

Noi painted, forgetting about being afraid, keeping the image of the elephant steady within her.

When Kun Ya woke up, Noi showed her the brown umbrella, twirling it slowly in the gloom of the rainy afternoon. Kun Ya reached out, her hand hovering over the elephant, never touching the silk, but tracing the shapes that Noi had painted. "Someday soon, Noi, you'll be selling these umbrellas."

Noi's heart beat faster, as though it would strike its way out of her chest. She couldn't speak a word.

"It may look as though I'm just sleeping, Noi, but I'm thinking, too." Kun Ya pressed her hand against her temple. "Paint whenever you can, while you can."

How could Kun Ya have known about the conversation with Mr. Poonsub, about Noi's new hopes, about how the elephant had appeared in her heart, inviting her to paint him?

"I will, Kun Ya. I'll paint after school, and when it rains, I will paint all day."

So every afternoon, and on rainy mornings, Noi painted. Often, she practiced on pieces of paper before painting on the umbrellas themselves.

One morning when the rain fell as though the sky was made of water, and lightning had knocked out the power so they had to light the lanterns, Kun Ya lifted a mangosteen in her palm and held it out to Noi. Noi moved as though to take the round, purple fruit, but Kun Ya said, "No, I just want you to see it."

Noi sat back and studied the mangosteen. Then, when she no longer heard the rain crashing on the roof or felt her own body or saw Kun Ya's thin hand, when only the round fruit existed, she reached for the paintbrush.

Kun Ya held the mangosteen steadily while Noi mixed paint to capture the exact purple of the skin. She combined red and more and more blue, red again, then black. She held the brush full of color close to the mangosteen to compare the purples.

Kun Ya nodded and Noi moved the brush toward the paper.

But Kun Ya said, "Wait, Noi. To make the fruit round, watch how the light falls on it. The purple here"—she touched the side closer to the lantern—"has a touch of white." She ran her finger along the other side of the mangosteen. "And here it casts a shadow, and the shadow runs up onto the skin."

Noi made two more puddles of color and added white to one, more black to the other.

As she began to paint on the rough white paper, Noi noticed that there were more shades of purple in the skin than she had first seen. She added a touch of yellow, and even green.

When at last Noi laid down her brush, Kun Ya relaxed her arm and let the mangosteen drop to her lap.

Noi sighed and stretched her fingers, becoming aware once more that she was in Kun Ya's room and that it was still raining outside. She glanced back and forth at what she'd painted and at the purple globe in Kun Ya's lap. "My painting doesn't look like the fruit at all," she said. How could that be? She'd felt so close to the mangosteen as she'd worked, almost as though she'd become it.

"Of course they don't look alike, Noi. This"— Kun Ya touched the mangosteen — "is only a mangosteen. While this"—she laid a finger on Noi's paper —"is the mangosteen plus you."

Noi hadn't thought of that. She smiled a little.

"And now." Kun Ya split open the tough violet skin to reveal the startling white segments within.

Although the fruit appeared completely white, Noi saw that the white contained touches of yellow and gray.

"Just notice for now," said Kun Ya. "You're tired already." She split the sections apart and handed one to Noi.

Noi took a bite of the sweet fruit.

When Ting came home that night, Noi took her into Kun Ya's room and closed the door. Noi unfurled her painted umbrellas one by one.

"Oh," Ting said at the sight of a bird swooping down from a flowering tree. Her face looked dreamy, as though she recalled her years of helping Kun Ya with the umbrellas.

"You could have done the same," said Noi.

"I don't think so, Noi. Show them to Kun Mere. Then she'll know how good you are and she may not send you to the factory. You can make money with these."

Again, Noi's heart beat faster. How had Ting guessed? Noi put her finger to her lips. "Not yet. She mustn't know yet." She worried that Ting, like Kun Ya, was perhaps too eager to like the umbrellas.

❋ Twelve

As the jungle began to dry out, Kun Pa went to work again laying bricks. At night he played his wooden flute, the notes slipping like water running through the house. Kun Mere's sewing machine no longer lost power.

Kun Ya still complained that her hands hurt and stayed in her room, but Noi began to paint outside, going off by herself to the clearing.

"You should sell the umbrellas," Ting kept insisting. "They're pretty. Make some money."

One night she added, "Please hurry, Noi. Another girl, only twelve years old, came today. She didn't cry, though. If you cry, your eyes get sore and you can't see the parts well."

Ting switched off the light, and the darkness leaped close. She laid a hand on Noi's forearm. "Please think about it."

"I think of nothing else," Noi said. "How can you bear the factory? Isn't the work hard for you, Ting?"

"Sometimes. But not always. Kun Mere lets me keep a little of the money I earn. I may buy you something soon."

Noi stayed silent. She couldn't tell Ting that no present could make her forget the sight of her at work in the factory.

♦ ♦ ♦

"Ting is getting too tired," Kun Ya said gently from time to time.

"She'll become used to it," Kun Mere always responded.

Each time Kun Ya protested, Kun Mere frowned. Her wrinkled forehead looked like a pool of water disturbed by a breeze.

The harvest got under way. On the walk home from school, Noi saw men and women cutting the rice with scythes and beating the long stems to release the grains. With harvest, preparations for the festival of Loy Krathong were beginning.

She began to walk faster, as though by hurrying, she could make the festival arrive sooner.

"Loy Krathong is coming, Ting," Noi reminded her one night.

"I'll have to work, you know."

"On Loy Krathong?" Noi couldn't believe that anyone would work on a festival day.

"Even on Loy Krathong. It's not so bad, Noi. I'm sure they'll let us play a radio."

One day Noi spotted a pickup truck inching down the jungle lane in front of the house. The bed was loaded with earthen lights to sell. "He's here, Kun Mere!" she shouted.

Kun Mere descended the ladder with her small purse of coins, Noi climbing down after her.

The man counted out the one hundred and sixty-one lights, setting them two by two in rows on the soft ground.

"I want to pay for my own this year," said Noi. From her pocket she drew eleven of the coins she'd earned with Kun Ya.

Another day the man returned with *kome*— paper lanterns that would hang in the trees and doorways.

"Which one?" Kun Mere asked Noi.

Noi touched the lanterns of translucent paper and the long streamers, the colors entering her body. Each color produced a different sensation: The yellow expanded inside her like a flower blooming, the pink fluttered, the dark green created a feeling of woody texture. The lanterns were all so beautiful that Noi had a hard time choosing.

The man began to fold the *kome* and wrap them back in the cellophane.

"Choose," Kun Mere urged, moving so close that Noi could feel her breath on the back of her neck.

"It's hard...."

Kun Mere's face suddenly softened with a

smile. "I know you love colors, Noi," she said. "Colors make you look so happy." She slipped her arm around Noi's shoulders, then lifted up a lantern shaped like a lotus, with long paper streamers of red, purple, and gold. "How about this?"

"Yes, that's the one." Noi put the lantern inside where it wouldn't get wet. That night, she dreamed she heard the sounds of Loy Krathong music.

✸ Thirteen

On the morning of Loy Krathong, Noi knelt next to Kun Mere in front of the charcoal stove. Ting had left early, as usual, for the factory.

"I feel so sad that Ting isn't with us," Noi said. Tears stung her eyes.

Kun Mere glanced at Noi, then looked back down at the blue-and-red flames licking the burning charcoal. "She's not as unhappy about it as you are, Noi."

What Kun Mere said was true, Noi had to admit. Somehow she just couldn't understand her sister.

"Don't be too sad for Ting," added Kun Mere.

As Noi watched the bean curd cook in a sticky sauce, she dried her cheeks with the back of her hand. She reminded herself that on Loy Krathong, prayers were more powerful. Maybe the spirits of water would listen and send Ting home. Or not. Maybe Kun Mere was right. Maybe Ting wanted to stay and earn more money.

When the house was in order, Noi examined her face in the water in the tall black jar in the bathroom. Next Loy Krathong, who would she see inside the jar? A factory worker or a painter of umbrellas?

She broke the surface of the water with the

dipper, shattering her face into fragments. When she'd finished bathing, she dressed herself in a sarong decorated with the same butterflies she loved to paint. The night before, she'd pressed her festival clothes using the iron full of charcoal from the stove. She'd pressed Ting's, too, just in case.

On the kitchen table, she packed clumps of sticky rice with thin slices of mango for the temple monks. She poured coconut milk with ground peanuts on top.

Kun Mere placed a hibiscus in Noi's hair. Noi felt the hard stem behind her ear. She knew the flower flared open, soft lavender with white streaks, but still she felt the bite of the stem.

♦ ♦ ♦

Kun Mere and Kun Pa walked ahead down the path through the jungle. Kun Mere wore her festival sarong and Kun Pa his good shirt with the high collar and soft loops of fabric that fastened in front.

Kun Ya and Noi followed, Kun Ya pointing out the different shades of the green leaves. "A lot of blue in that green, a little more yellow in that," she said.

On Loy Krathong the world seemed new and gleaming, as though anything could happen. Everyone moved quickly toward the pointed spire of the glittering temple emerging through the trees.

Boys and girls slid along the stone dragons that wound down each side of the temple steps. The tiger cat leaped down from one of the dragons to greet Noi.

Noi recalled how, when they were little, she and Ting had slid down the dragons, too, sometimes tearing their clothes on the rough stone. She still felt like sliding down those dragons, but probably Ting, now that she was grown up with a job, wouldn't find it fun.

Kriamas arrived on a tiny motorcycle, riding behind her mother and father, blowing kisses to Noi and other friends.

Under the heavy shade of giant teak trees, villagers had set up tables and spread out silver earrings, miniature Buddhas, and embroidered silk cloths on tables to sell.

Noi carried two of her coins.

She handed the first coin to a man with cages of tiny birds he'd caught in the jungle. She chose a cage and undid the hook. With a flutter, the bird darted out. As Noi watched it disappear into the sky, she pictured Ting escaping her confinement.

But perhaps Ting didn't *want* that, Noi reminded herself. Instead she imagined herself flying freely like the bird, free in the jungle instead of caged in a factory.

She gave a woman the other *baht* in exchange for a bit of soft gold paste.

With her fingers closed over the gold, Noi climbed the steps. She slipped off her sandals and entered the temple.

A golden Buddha towered so high that his head touched the roof. Like all Thai Buddhas, he had the eyes of a deer, a chin like a mango seed, hair like a scorpion's stingers, and hands like lotus blossoms about to open.

Standing on tiptoe, Noi just reached the top of a giant foot. She rubbed the gold from her fingertips onto one of the toes while she pictured herself standing forever in the golden sunlight of the jungle.

Surrounded by sweet-smelling, white *kasalong* flowers, the monks chanted the wise words of the Buddha.

Noi stood in line behind the villagers carrying bowls of fat bananas, slippery white rambutan fruits, and thick curries. Everyone placed the food before the row of monks.

After Noi offered her own dish of sticky rice and mango, she bowed low three times, then pressed her forehead to the floor and closed her eyes.

After the monks had eaten, the villagers spread out the rest of the food on mats and gathered in small groups to eat together.

"May I sit with you?" Kriamas asked.

Noi smiled and motioned toward the mat.

Kriamas settled herself, placing her plate of food in front of her. Even though Kriamas had a year and a half left of elementary school, she was already making plans for her future. "My parents talked with my aunt and uncle in Bangkok. I'll be staying with them while I go to school."

Noi took a long drink of water.

"You're so quiet, Noi. Aren't you happy for me?"

"Of course I'm happy." Noi felt quiet because she couldn't bring herself to talk about her future with Kriamas. Kriamas was so sure of her own destiny and so satisfied with it, while worry tore away at Noi's heart. Sometimes her heart felt like a seed stripped of its fruit.

To shield herself from Kriamas and her questioning, Noi began to tuck some of her food into a bowl to take to Ting. The curried fish and dish of small, round Thai eggplant had been blessed by the temple monks and was now holy food that would bring good luck to whoever ate it.

❈ Fourteen

A green glow fell gently through the jungle canopy.

Kun Pa sliced fresh banana leaves off the tree with a knife. As his face moved in and out of the light and shade, Noi felt her heart shift. Probably Kun Pa missed Ting today, too.

Kun Pa finished cutting and tossed the leaves onto the table underneath the house.

He sat down on a bench, his long knife across his knees.

While Noi tore the leaves into strips, Kun Mere and Kun Ya wove the strips with quick fingers, forming them into baskets.

Curious, the pigs and chickens came close. The rooster hopped up onto the worktable.

"Down," said Kun Mere, knocking him back.

"But, Kun Mere, he just wants to look," said Noi. "You've hurt his feelings."

"He can look when we're finished."

"He wants you to paint him," joked Kun Ya, brushing her forehead with the back of her hand. "He'd look nice on red silk."

Noi giggled. "He does look as if he's posing. But let me make Ting's *krathong*."

Kun Ya handed her a pile of strips, and Noi wove them into a tight basket that wouldn't leak. She concentrated on making the basket strong and even enough to hold Ting's candle without tipping.

If the candle stayed lit until the *krathong* floated out of sight on the river, wishes would come true. What would Ting wish for? Noi didn't know anymore.

After Noi had tucked the last end of banana leaf into place, Kun Ya leaned over to put a white orchid with a yellow center inside the *krathong*. Noi added a stick of incense and a white candle.

As she worked, Noi felt constantly on the verge of turning to Ting to share a joke, to giggle, to show her the half-made *krathong*. Ting's absence sunk into her as a stone falls slowly through water.

She set to work on her own *krathong*. One minute she felt herself wishing, as though what she wanted could never come true; the next minute dreaming, as though it already had.

Snip snip, went the sewing scissors, and Kun Mere laid the bits of Noi's black hair in her *krathong*.

Then Kun Mere took Noi's hand. She cut off a crescent of fingernail and placed that, too, in Noi's basket.

Sending old, useless bits of hair and fingernail down the river symbolized letting go of old, useless things in life and making room for the new. *What would be the new?* Noi wondered.

Kun Pa dropped a tiny fifty-*stang* coin into each *krathong,* concluding the making of the baskets.

As the sunlight fell lower on the tree trunks, Noi suddenly heard the pad of footsteps. She turned to see Ting running through the jungle, the shadows of leaves splashing across her face.

"They let us go early today," she announced, breathing as though she'd run all the way from the bus stop.

Kun Pa got up from the bench so quickly that the knife clattered to the ground.

Kun Mere set down the *krathong* she was weaving, and it fell apart into strips again.

Kun Ya held out her arms and Ting slowed her dash to move into the embrace.

Ting home after all! The Buddha had listened!

When Kun Ya released Ting, Noi stepped forward. "Here." She placed Ting's *krathong* into her hands, the banana smell fragrant between them. She felt as though she, too, had been running.

"Oh, thank you," said Ting. Her chest rose and fell with her breath.

"I'm so happy," whispered Noi.

"Yes. It was nice of them to close the factory early."

They all sat on the bench in a row, saying nothing, Ting holding her *krathong* in her lap. Noi watched beams of light arcing pink and dusky onto the forest floor, feeling herself grow rose-colored inside.

"Why don't you two light the *phang patit?*" asked Kun Mere finally, holding up a small box of matches.

Yes, it is time, thought Noi. Every year she and Ting lit the lamps together.

"Let's outline the path with the lights," Ting suggested.

"And if there's some left over, we can put them under the trees."

They began to light the one hundred and sixty-one lamps, each a tiny flame of gratitude to the Buddha. For Noi, each strike of the match also represented a tiny request: *Let me be a painter!*

The pigs followed, sniffing at the lamps.

Kun Mere hung the lotus-shaped lantern from a branch, the streamers rippling in the breeze.

❋ Fifteen

The night of Loy Krathong, the night of the twelfth full moon, carried the first crisp hint of winter.

Kun Ya walked hesitantly, as though the cold air had gotten into her knees.

Noi held one of her arms, Ting the other, dressed in the festival clothes that Noi had ironed. Kun Pa and Kun Mere went ahead, talking softly.

"Look, Kun Ya." Noi pointed out a cluster of earthen lanterns under the trees, the hanging lanterns close to the houses.

"And look," said Kun Ya. She pointed to the *hinghoy* bobbing in and out of the trees, as though they, too, were celebrating.

When the path led into a clearing near the river, the *kome loy*, huge, soft, orange lanterns, floated freely in the sky. Noi saw the flicker of the fires that heated and lifted them. As the *kome* drifted away, so would bad luck.

Could those beautiful lanterns save *her* from bad luck? Noi wondered. Or was it just a foolish belief? In spite of all the ceremony, next year might she, too, come running from the factory when Loy Krathong was almost over?

As the path widened and joined another path, Kun Pa and Kun Mere greeted villagers on their way to the river, *sawasdees* rippling into the cold air.

Noi smelled the sweet, earthy river plants. Here and there, people were lighting their candles. The full moon rose over the horizon like a coin of good fortune. *Krathong* had already been set free, the dark shapes of the floating baskets and the tiny flames reflected in the golden, moonlit water.

"Listen, Ting." Noi shivered with excitement. "People must be dancing. I hear a big drum and tiny cymbals."

A boy chased a girl on the other side of the river, their giggles bouncing through the cold air. Another couple sat close under a low-hanging tree.

Noi stared into the current alive with flames. The spirits of water lived here — especially tonight.

She felt Kun Pa's sleeve brush hers.

"You go first, Noi."

"Oh, let someone else...," she started to say.

"I'll come with you," Kun Ya said softly.

With one hand, Noi held the *krathong* with its precious cargo, and with the other, she supported Kun Ya's arm, steadying her. Damp grass brushed against Noi's legs as she walked to the river. The touch was like the caress of the river spirits.

When they knelt together on the bank, Noi sensed her family standing behind her. Kun Pa leaned over her shoulder and struck a match, and Noi shielded the flame with her hands. First he lit the incense stick. The sweet smoke spiraled into the air. Then he touched the flame to the wick of the candle, holding it until the flame transferred itself.

Noi set the *krathong* on the water, balanced

it, and, with a quick flutter of her hands, pushed it away from the bank.

"Mae Nam," Mother Water, Noi whispered. She prayed that the basket would float on this river until it reached the larger river downstream. If the *krathong* arrived at that wide current, surely her dreams would come true.

"Mae Nam," echoed Kun Ya.

The basket began its journey on the golden water. The *krathong* got caught in an eddy and swirled around three times before heading downstream.

When it joined the others, Noi suddenly couldn't tell which was hers. She rose up on tiptoe, trying to fix her eyes on the tiny flame.

When the basket had surely gone, merged forever with the other *krathong*, Noi turned to see the golden moonlight reflected in Kun Ya's eyes.

"You can't do anymore tonight, little daughter. Your *krathong* is in the hands of the river spirits now."

Yet Noi couldn't help looking over the luminous water again, searching for a promising sign.

❈ Sixteen

The next morning, Kun Mere handed Noi a silver bowl with designs on the sides. It was full of rice and bits of crispy dried fish.

Noi took the food and went down the ladder outside the house, balancing the bowl carefully with one hand.

Three monks strolled down the lane in bright robes the color of the sun rising behind them. Noi noticed the way the orange stood out against the green background of banana leaves and vines climbing up the coconut palms. Each monk carried a large silver bowl.

Noi bowed to them, kneeling on the soft dirt. As the monks held out their bowls, she spooned the food in, carefully dividing it into three equal portions.

After the monks had moved on to the next house, Noi stayed kneeling. She opened herself to the trilling calls of the birds, the breeze lifting the hairs around her forehead, to the lemony feel of the early sunlight.

When she rose, she approached the spirit house underneath the big tree. The spirit house was a miniature building raised to eye level on a single pole. Kun Mere had already lit incense here and laid out flowers and food. Instead of a Buddha, the shrine housed an Indian yogi

115

with a long beard, a water buffalo, and a farmer wearing a big round hat.

Once Noi had asked Kun Ya why all Thai families had both a Buddha altar and a spirit house.

Kun Ya had taken a moment to think. Then she'd leaned forward and said, "Do you remember, Noi, when Srithon's oldest son was sick? Srithon prayed to the spirits. But when it looked as if the son might die, Srithon went to the temple to pray. He prayed to the Buddha that his son would have a good transition between lives."

Noi moved the farmer closer to the water buffalo and the yogi behind the fresh orchid flower. They led such simple lives here in the spirit house, as did the monks who wandered the road in their daily ritual of begging food.

Which could understand her complicated worries? She wondered if she should carry those worries to the Buddha who lived on the altar, or to the spirits who lived all about her.

"Here, Noi." Kun Mere handed her a pineapple as she was leaving for school. "Remember, Kun Kru asked you to bring one today."

Noi took the pineapple under her arm and cradled it, the prickly skin against her own, the spikes of the leaves against her neck.

In the afternoon, Kun Kru asked the children to place their pineapples on the desks. The room smelled sweet.

Even the boys had brought pineapples. If the school had been bigger, the boys would have gone with a male teacher to learn how to weave fans or baskets out of bamboo. But since there was only Kun Kru, they, too, learned how to carve fruit.

Kun Kru held up a photograph of a pineapple shaped like a bird. Then she took her own pineapple and sliced off the skin, the tough diamond shapes falling to the table. With quick, practiced strokes, Kun Kru transformed the yellow block of fruit into a feathery bird. The room smelled even sweeter.

When Kun Kru finished, Noi and the others took out their pocketknives and set to work.

Noi cut carefully, making sure that her knife didn't slip. She enjoyed the different shades of yellow inside the pineapple, including the pale, almost white, streaks. She felt saturated with the golden colors. The juice stickied her fingers.

"It's coming along nicely, Noi," Kun Kru

commented as she circulated among the students, helping guide a knife or make a suggestion.

At the end of the afternoon, Kun Kru displayed all of the carvings on a large table. The birds looked crisp and delicate, as though they would bring goodness to whoever ate them.

Yet flies were beginning to circle the pineapples.

Suddenly, Noi recalled Ting bringing home a watermelon carved into the shape of a swan, even the green-and-white rind part of the design. Everyone had gathered to admire the swan's long, arched neck, its perfect wings.

But that skill was of no benefit to Ting now. While the other children wrapped their pineapples to take home, Noi decided to leave hers behind for the flies.

✸ Seventeen

The next day as Noi and Kun Mere were scattering vegetable peelings for the chickens, Mr. Subsin came down the path on a motorcycle instead of in his truck. When he stopped, he put his feet on the ground but didn't get off the motorcycle. "I can't buy any more mosquito nets until the next rainy season," he announced. "The villagers in every direction have enough for now."

"What about the ones I've already made?" asked Kun Mere.

"Keep them. I'll be back next season."

Noi glanced quickly at Kun Mere. She was staring down at Mr. Subsin's feet—one on the ground, the other balanced on the pedal.

After Mr. Subsin roared back to town, leaving the bushes shaking on either side of the path, Noi watched Kun Mere climb slowly up the ladder into the house. Noi followed her through the big front room and into the kitchen.

Kun Mere took a head of garlic and began to break off the cloves, cracking them loose with more force than usual.

"Will there be enough money now?" Noi asked.

Kun Mere flattened a clove with the side of a heavy knife, releasing the strong garlic scent into the kitchen. "It will be harder to buy what we need."

Noi slipped into Kun Ya's room, where the umbrellas were stacked in the corners. She knew the paintings by heart. She rested her hand on a pale green umbrella and recalled how she'd sat in the forest when the rain had paused, watching a family of chipmunks climbing in and out of their holes or skittering along branches, their fluffy tails raised like flags behind them. Sometimes she closed her eyes and sensed the way the little animals traveled— the darts and then the careful pauses, the darts again. When she understood the chipmunks, she'd painted three, their nervous movements in every stroke of her brush. Even after she'd finished the painting, she'd lived the rest of the day with the feeling of the chipmunks' scurries inside her.

She wasn't sure that Mr. Poonsub would accept the umbrellas, but the time had come to see. He might look at one and laugh, his heavy stomach moving up and down. He might treat her like a child playing at selling umbrellas. Even the women might scoff at her childish work.

But she couldn't wait any longer. If her painting proved good enough to make money for Kun Mere, then surely Kun Mere would let her be an artist.

Noi found Kun Pa underneath the house, sharpening his long knife with a stone. She waited until he had finished and replaced the knife into its wooden sheath. Then she spoke: "Kun Pa, will you take me to the tourist market on Saturday?"

"We have no money to buy anything, Noi," he replied.

"No, I mean to sell something."

He looked at her with his thin eyebrows lifted.

"Kun Ya has been too tired to paint umbrellas, so I've been painting them for her," Noi continued. Would he be worried that she'd spoiled expensive umbrellas and used up the paints?

"Well, let's see, then," Kun Pa finally said.

Noi climbed the ladder, then entered the house and Kun Ya's room. She selected the brown umbrella with the elephant on it, opening it partway to make certain it was the one she wanted. In the gloom, it cast a rich, bronze light.

"That's an especially beautiful one, Noi."

Noi turned to see Kun Ya leaning up on her elbow in bed. "I thought you were asleep. I'm going to show this umbrella to Kun Pa."

"I'm so glad, Noi."

Kun Pa met her at the ladder. As he climbed up, Noi unfurled the umbrella. The elephant sprang to life, filled with vigor, reaching forward with its trunk to Kun Pa.

That evening after dinner, Kun Pa said, "Bring out the elephant umbrella again, Noi. Show the others."

Noi carried the umbrella into the living room, where everyone still sat around the eating mat. Just before she opened it, she looked at Kun Ya, who nodded slightly. After she had set the umbrella on its side on the floor, there was a long pause until Kun Mere said, "Where are the others? Your father says you have more."

So Noi brought out all the painted umbrellas. She went back and forth to Kun Ya's room to carry them one by one, springing them open when she entered the living room. The silk petals spread in the jungle night, under the light from the bare bulb. Soon the umbrellas rested like a company of proud flowers in the living room.

As Noi looked at the umbrellas, she traced her journey from one to the next: that day the flock of small blue birds; or the day of bright sun mixed with dark rain, the playful monkey in the tree... The umbrellas told the story of her life these past months.

Kun Pa nodded and laughed in short

bursts of happiness as Noi revealed each painting.

Ting and Kun Ya smiled at each other as Noi's secrets came to light.

"Oh, Noi," said Kun Mere over and over. After the last one was brought out, she said, "I knew you loved color, little daughter. I just didn't know how much."

Although market day was sunny and warm, Noi grew cold as Kun Pa wheeled the tricycle between the stalls to Mr. Poonsub's booth.

The women teased her as usual, begging her to sell to them instead. "Just this once," cried one. "Where is your grandmother?" asked another.

"At home," Noi called back. A wave of

sadness passed over her. Kun Ya should be with her now.

Finally, Kun Pa stopped the *samlaw* in front of Mr. Poonsub's table stacked high with Thai silks.

"At last," Mr. Poonsub said to Noi. "I haven't seen you in a long time."

"Kun Ya is still tired."

"Again, I'm sorry," he said, reaching for a pale lavender umbrella. He unfurled it, examining the delicate painting of a tree arching over a rice field, and then opened a yellow one. "Did your grandmother paint these?"

Noi felt her heart drop like a ripe mango falling from a tree. "No, Mr. Poonsub. I did."

He opened one umbrella after another and left them spread, reflecting colors onto the bundles of silks.

Noi thought that Mr. Poonsub must be

searching for an umbrella that he liked. Surely, she'd ruined them! Kun Ya and the others had been too kind to tell her. Or maybe Kun Ya's eyesight had gone bad.

Noi felt shame spread over her, a redness as from a bleeding cut. She looked down at her feet in their dusty sandals. She sensed Kun Pa behind her, folding and unfolding his hands.

"Hmmm. These umbrellas do look different. But good in their way. The painting is fresh and lively," Mr. Poonsub said at last. "You've inherited your grandmother's gift."

Noi let her breath out.

"Will you buy them, then?" Kun Pa stepped forward.

Without answering, Mr. Poonsub turned to his cash box and counted paper money and two ten-*baht* coins into Noi's hands. "And a little extra for pocket money"— he counted out a few more coins —"until next Saturday."

When they turned the corner, out of sight of Mr. Poonsub, Noi cried, "Oh, Kun Pa. He even wants to buy more!"

"Such a wonderful day!" Kun Pa hugged Noi close to him and laughed.

"And now, here's this for Kun Mere," said Noi when Kun Pa let her go. Carefully, she placed the bills with the coins on top into Kun Pa's hands.

"This is yours." Kun Pa handed back the pocket money. He put the rest in his embroidered money bag, then touched her cheek with his fingertips. "Your money will more than make up for that lost from mosquito nets."

Kun Pa let Noi climb into the empty tricycle basket for the trip home. He pedaled down the busy streets and then onto the road into the countryside. They passed under a tree of trumpet flowers, the heavy blooms hanging downward.

"Please go back to that tree," Noi asked, turning around in the basket.

Kun Pa circled and stopped.

Noi put her face right underneath one of the creamy trumpets. The inside blushed with pink. She ran her finger over the ruffled edge and breathed in a subtle, musky scent. She closed her eyes until she could feel the flower inside her.

Tomorrow she would paint the trumpet flower on a pure white umbrella. She couldn't wait to show Kun Ya.

Glossary

baht: Thai coin worth about five U.S. cents

farang: Caucasian foreigner

hinghoy: firefly

kasalong: white flowers

kome: paper lanterns

kome loy: floating lanterns

krathong: basket

Kun Kru: Teacher

Kun Mere: Mother

Kun Pa: Father

Kun Ya: Grandmother

Loy Krathong: Harvest Festival (literally "Floating Baskets")

Mae Nam: Mother Water

mangosteen: a dark purple fruit with white inside

phang patit: earthen lamps

rambutan: a bright red fruit with white inside

samlaw: a large tricycle

sarong: a rectangular length of fabric used as a garment

sawasdee: *hello* and *goodbye*

stang: Thai coin worth about one-fiftieth of a U.S. cent

ACKNOWLEDGMENTS

I would like to acknowledge Kanlaya Yaiprasan, whose work inspired this book; my husband, Panratt Manoorasada, who contributed generously to the story during its long evolution; Kruamas Woodtikarn, who assisted with cultural details; Gretchen Will Mayo, who shed light on the inner life of the artist; Irma Sheppard, who lovingly helped with the revision; and my editors, Amy Ehrlich and Deborah Wayshak, whose vision and insight guided my search for the story's heart.

ALSO BY CAROLYN MARSDEN

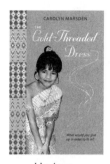

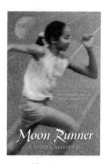

Hardcover
ISBN 978-0-7636-1569-7

Hardcover
ISBN 978-0-7636-2635-8

Hardcover
ISBN 978-0-7636-2117-9

Paperback
ISBN 978-0-7636-2993-9

Paperback
ISBN 978-0-7636-3304-2

co-written with
Virginia Shin-Mui Loh

Hardcover
ISBN 978-0-7636-3175-8

Hardcover
ISBN 978-0-7636-3012-6